COLLEGE MAN

COLLEGE MAN

NITA ELSE

ISBN: 978-1-952302-96-1 (sc)
ISBN: 978-1-952302-97-8 (e)

Library of Congress Control Number: 2021919640

Acknowledgement

Thank you to all my supporters and fans. Thank you Jesus. Also Thank you to soon to be fans and followers. Thank You [Mom} Rosie Else for believing in me. Thank You to Dominque, Denita, Demarcus and grandbabies, I Love you all. Thanks for the patience while I ventured this journey. Thank You Nikki[my sister] and #1 FAN. More to come for ya'll enjoyment. Thank You Mr. Sherman for the photo. To my old and new fans Nothing But UP From Here. Thank You!

Chapter One

The College Man

The week seemed as if it flew by. Poet thought.

"The family reunion will begin friday afternoon. I have everything I need to kick it off just right." Poet remarked to her mom.

"You need to get our carry chairs. Or we'll be playing musical chairs all weekend. I have no intention of standing the whole weekend." Poet's mom Rosa replied. "Mom calm down with all of the excitement and cooking, you won't be worried about a chair. Besides your name is written on your chair.

"Everyone knows not to sit in it!" Poet explained. "Mom I'll be there at 4 pm, be ready. This reunion is about to go down. Talk to you later." "Goodbye."

Poet said placing the phone on the hook.

After work on Friday, Poet Ellis prepared herself for the first day of her reunion. Her black hair was soft, curly, and draped her faced. Poet stood less than five feet, thick as forty weight gravy. Her medium chocolate skin was smooth, and her deep brown eyes shined behind Crystal Berteer frames. Blowing the horn for her mom, Poet stood outside the car for one last opinion about her choice of clothing.

"You look ok, Come get these things. We are running late." Her mom replied. Poet threw her head back laughing loudly. "You don't look so bad yourself." They both wore last years gold reunion shirt with denim knee knockers.

Poet wore heels and her mom flats, both black. The yard was full already as they pulled in.

Poet immediately set everything together. Everyone loved their food. Fried fish, chicken, and shrimp. "Oh yeah its on and poppin!" Poet yelled.

The family danced and sang out loud to the Cha Cha, Slide song.

"Teach me that." Someone screamed. Scampering to the concrete slab full of people.

"Hold this dipper while I show these folks how it's done." Poet remarked, handing the utensil to a cousin who was waiting on the delights.

"Go Poet, Go Poet!" Someone screamed as she gyrating into the air. Poet smiled big showing a single gold and whites.

Poet walked back to her chair, wiping sweat, blowing quick breathes. "Its been a minute since I did any dancing. I'm rusty." She explained.

Fanning herself with her hand. Poet caught a glimpse of a man walking up the hill. As he topped the hill there were two other men not far behind.

"Damn, ! Who does he belong to." One of the older ladies cackled with glee.

Getting them to all look at the men. One of them Short and stocky had a shirt that said Chanel's Daddy, spray painted across the front.

"Oh, That's Rene's baby daddy. But who are the others." An aunt asked.

"I can't say." Poet replied. " Looks as if we are about to find out, here they come."

"This is my mom Poet, and these are my great aunts and cousins." Rene explained introducing the men Rene said. "This is Robert, Roger,

and Antwon. My boyfriend and his brothers from Oregon."

"Hello," everyone spoke and began to chatter and whisper. The men all seemed to be in a foreign land. They were from Portland, Oregon now standing in country Longville, Texas.

"Do they have any uncles? They look a little young to me." One of the older women replied. The men laughed and all began to indulge in the festivities.

As Poet rose to return to cooking, she felt eyes upon her. She glanced around the yard trying to see who's staring her down.

It was Antwon. Poet looked back at the cooking pot. Not long though, she couldn't stop taking memory photos of Antwon.

She caught herself daydreaming about him in all his glory.

Antwon was very muscular. The Burberry long sleeve shirt in summer hide nothing. Neither did the creased black and faded out Tommy Lama's jeans.

Damn he is fine as hell. Look at his long braided hair. Heaven has sent an eye blessing. Poet thought.

Poet switched her eyes away when he caught her looking. Sipping from his cup Antwon gave it a little salute. As if saying, I see you to shawty.

The night grew cool and people were thinning out. Poet lost track of things while serving more food. When she looked up Antwon and the other men were gone.

Damn I missed. Poet thought as she scanned the yard.

"Mom, If you don't mind, Would you fix three to go's please. With everything on them." Rene cried out. Upon finishing the last plate, Antwon appeared before her.

"Thank you for allowing us to crash the party. It's been a blast. Espccially seeing you." Antwon remarked sensually.

Was that a flirtatious remark Poet thought to herself, handing him the plates. He smiles said "Thank You" and walked away.

Chapter One\Half

Tea To Pour

Poet's weekend was off the chain. The reunion lasted all weekend. She thought about the handsome man she met on Friday! She dreamed about him and her basking in glory. But why, she only saw him once. She pictured him naked standing in front of her. In her mind she conversed with him. She could hear his voice in her ear. Hell she even wet her panties thinking of what sex with him would be like. She wanted to ask Rena about him. But she didn't want her daughter to know she was fantasizing about him. Poet knew he was young. She also knew there was no way in the world she could be with this young man. Damn he's on the brain she thought…

Poet had been single for a while now. She admitted to herself. She needed a man in her life. Work and home was all she knew. She sat and ate alone every night. Her routine was getting old and so was she.

"Girl, I got tea to pour. Did you see the young guy that came to the reunion with Rena's baby daddy. He was so handsome. I couldn't take my eyes off of him." Poet told her favorite cousin Ann.

"I sure did notice him, Tony was stuck so close I couldn't move around. I definetly peeped hard though." Ann said giggling.

"Well what about I'm having hot dreams about him. I need a life. Hell last week I had a dream about Micheal Ealy." Poet replied laughing.

"You sure have dick on the brain girl get you some before you go crazy.

Maybe you should get a vibrator." Ann remarked.

"Well I'm going to have to do something. My oil surely needs to be changed.

That's for certain. Well I'll talk to you later. The boss is breathing down my ass." Poet told her.

"OK, Later girl, get you some. Ha, Ha!" Ann said hanging up.

The rest of the day Poet tried to keep busy. Keep her mind off sex. Nothing seemed to help.

Chapter Two

Call Me

Rene entered her moms front door. "Mom Antwon wants your phone number.

He likes you. He says you are breath taking." She spilled out.

"Antwon is not serious, he's bullshitting. How old is he anyway." Poet asked.

"Twenty-one," Rene replied. "Mom he asked me about you all weekend. What did you say to him?"

"Nothing, I was nice to him and everyone else. I made no difference in the people there. Just being myself." Poet remarked smiling.

"Well I did not give him the number. I figured he will be alright. Besides he's in college and you are thirty-five. What could you all possibly have in common anyway." Rene blurred.

"If you only knew," Poet muttered "If only you knew. I'm not going to loose my head over a little tail. I know he wasn't talking about me." Poet replied.

About two weeks passed. Poet continued to think about Antwons and the conversation with her daughter. Could he be serious? What did I miss? She thought. Her phone rang it was Rene. She had tea to pour!

"Mom Antwon asked me about you again. He 's getting on my nerves. All he talks about is you. How good you look, and smell.

He is driving me up a tree. He also asked me for your number again." Rene spoke shockingly.

"Did you give it to him?" Poet asked.

"No, I didn't. I figure he wants it so bad he can ask you himself." Rene cried.

"How will he do that. I won't see him again. We travel in different circles, besides he lives in Killeen. That's a good ride from here." Poet replied.

"Well he continues to ask for your number. What do I tell Him?" Rene asked flabbergasted.

"Give it to him." Poet remarked.

"Are you crazy he is fourteen years younger than you. What will ya'll talk about. Oh! never mind I will give it to him". Rene smirked.

"Thank you, I'll take care of the rest. Besides I only want to know what he wants with me?" Smiling inside and out Poet said.

About a week later Poet was hanging with friends when her phone alerted her of a text. It's him, Antwon. Poet secretly read the message.

With an ear to ear grin Poet turned her phone off.

The next morning Poet got to work early. She couldn't help but to read the text again. "Hello, I finally got you. I will be waiting for your response. Call me.

Mr. Sherman." Poet shook her head in amazing thought. How about that. A young man interested in me. What do I do.

HUMPP!

Chapter Two\Half

Lay And Wait

Poet couldn't think straight. This Man had been on her mind. And she had been on his mind. She would have never thought it. Now what. What would she do if he did call her.

What would they talk about. Shit anything they wanted to. She thought. She knew one thing for sure, she needed to find out had hell frozen over. She was confident about things in her life. But the thoughht of a twenty-one year old man was making her rethink somethings. Would they really hit it off. Now that she knew he was interested in her too. Would they really have steamy hot sex. Or would they just talk on the phone. Have a one night stand, or a full fledge relationship.

Damn Poet cool it. She thought. She thought he only wanted to talk. Don't over exert yourself. Let him call you. That's when you find out where his head is. She just had to lay and wait. Maybe something good was headed her way. Yes a HOT, Handsome, Fine specimen of a Man!

Chapter Three

Close Encounter

"Meet me somewhere." Antwon asked. Poet was almost speechless as she heard Antwon's voice on the other end of the phone line. " I would love to talk to you face to face. That way we can talk like we want." Antwon remarked.

After a moment Poet spoke. "OK."

"You name the place you are most comfortable. That way we have no distractions." Antwon spoke.

"OK." Poet repeated. "When do you have time?" She asked.

"No better time than the present. I can pick you up in fifteen minutes." He replied.

"I'll be ready." She said.

Checking herself in the long glass mirror. Poet smacked her own ass. You look great girl calm down. She thought.

"Hello," Antwon spoke smiling. While Poet entered his white trooper.

"Hello," Poet spoke back. "You look nice."

"Thank you, you do too babe. Where are we headed?" Antwon asked.

"To this quiet park a few blocks from here." She said.

Pulling away Poet caught a glimpse of Antwon checking her out. "Eyes on the road, Sir." Poet spoke aloud.

"I'm sorry I can't help it. when I'm in the presence of a good looking lady all I can do is stare." Antwon replied with a huge smile.

Antwon being a gentleman opened her door. He guided her to a bench under a brown wooded gazebo. It was all you could see on that side of the dark park. There shined a light from the far distance. Poet sat atop of the bench, Antwon stood in front of her.

"I'm grateful you said yes. I'm admiring your silhouette casting in the shadows.

Your probably wandering why I wanted to meet you."

"You, Your eyes spoke to me that day of the reunion. I had to see you. Meet with you alone. I assumed you wouldn't have taken me serious.

Had I said something in front of everyone. I couldn't get you out of my mind."

Antwon confessed.

Poet smiled as if saying... That's so sweet. "You do realize we have a huge age gap right. Why me?" She asked.

"Because you are beautiful, not to get beside myself." "But you are fine as an expensive bottle of wine. I listened to you talk. I thought, she's country but damn she looks good. I'm From Oregon, so you have to forgive me for the country remark. I'm still getting a custom with Texas. Please look over me."

Apologetically he spoke.

"Ha, Ha! She bellowed. "Your serious aren't you. You don't care about the age difference. Neither do I. I too consumed you, as your figure began to top that hill. My heart began to thump hard. I could barely stay focused. I too felt something strange." She replied.

"Where do you see yourself in five years?" He asked.

"Five years from now I plan on being married, have the house on the hill with the white picket fence. . I also plan on publishing a book or two." She explained!

"Your a writer, me too. I write poetry. I'm going to the NFL within three years. Ready to settle down some, get serious with the right lady.

Someone who needs me. Some of the young lady's are still immature. Not all of them, I am still looking. Yet I meet you, and it's not just about your body. It's also about your mind, I want to get to know a woman. Poet I am talking about you."

Antwon remarked.

Poet listened as she watched car lights passing.

"May I ask you a question?" Antwon asked.

"Ask away." She spoke looking in his direction."

"What kink of panties do u have on." He asked.

"Black lace hipster. Why?" Poet answered smirking.

"No disrespect, but your body is banging. I can't touch but a mental picture works wonders. Damn, I would love to be your sexual toy.

Let you teach me a thing or two.

Tasting you, giving you some of me. I don't mean to come on so strong, yet that's part of what I want with you."

"The other things are." Poet asked.

"I need someone who speaks with a rational head. A lady likes to be held after love making sex. I want to kiss you passionately, you cook real food.

I can enjoy these quality's in a woman. Those are things I look forward to experience with you, Poet." Antwon said.

"With me? You seem to know something I don't. We just meet. You see that far into the future." Poet asked while turning to look at Antwon.

In mid-air Antwon's lips met hers. A few seconds went by before Poet pulled away. She was flabbergasted.

"We could." Antwon whispered as he locked lips with Poet again. This time Poet didn't resist. She cautiously leaned into it. Antwon wrapped his arms around Poet's shoulders. Poet could feel his heart beating. Antwon's body language spoke loudly. His breathing was heavy. He even rubbed his left hand across Poet's face.

Then slowly through her soft hair. Poet melted in his arms. She had no intention of going to this point. But he wasn't about to stop now. Poet reached around Antwon as far she could. She began to kiss him deeply, grabbing his shirt in clinched fist. Damn this feels so good... Poet thought. The kiss seemed endless.

They finally pulled away.

"Whew! Poet blew. "Are you getting hot or is that just me?" She asked.

"No babe it's both of us. That kiss was wild. Your lips are soft and sweet. The touch of your warm body close to me is bothering the hell out of me." Antwon replied. As he sat down on the bench.

"Can I ask you another question?" He asked.

"You the law with all these questions." Poet remarked.

"No. I just wanted to know why you pulled away the first kiss." He replied quickly.

"Because I was caught off guard. I had no idea you were going to do that. She spoke.

"I like you Poet. I really like you. Now the box top opened. All awkwardness is over." Please take me serious. Antwon said as he pulled her onto his lap.

Poet straddled Antwon's legs. Antwon caressed her waist up and down. They looked other. Neither saw the car lights pulling into the parking lot.

"Hello." A voice called out as a male figure rounded the SUV.

"Its the police!" Poet remarked softly. She slide off Antwon's lap. They both sat side by side as if they were just talking.

The cop was so busy searching the truck. He never saw them sitting in the dark.

"Hello. Is there a problem officer?" Antwon called out.

"I didn't see you all there. The public parks closes at eleven p.m. Sir."

The officer explained as he shone his flashlight on them.

"We are sorry, we just wanted a quiet place to talk. Antwon replied.

"May I see id's please." He requested.

They both handed him their cards. He of course ran them. Poet Ellis, Antwon Sherman clear came over his shoulder C.B.

"Your Not who we are looking for. But you must leave this park, have a good night." The officer told them. He turned to leave talking into his C.B.

"Yeah their clear put their name on the list though." As he disappeared into his patrol car.

They both blew a sigh of relief.

"That was a close encounter, Poet. I can see you are already going to be trouble.

Now let me get you home." Antwon said grinning.

They both laughed aloud on the ride back to her house.

"May I kiss you one last time for good measure. After all you tried to get me arrested." Antwon cried.

"No." Poet replied playfully. She leaned across the seat, pecked Antwon on the lips and closed the door waving. Poet had the world's biggest smile on her face.

Her heart was off scale. Nerved from Antwon's kiss, the thought of the police rolling up on them. The fact she had just threw all caution to the wind.

Chapter Four

Keeping Me Up At Night

"Hello," the deep male voice spoke. "Are you busy. I need to talk. And your the only person who seems to understand me." Antwon said.

"Hello to you too, vent if you must. I'm all ears. Besides I have been thinking about you all day." Poet replied.

"My roommate told me an old friend came to the apartment. She said he had a gun. And he was looking for me. He told her he was pissed at me for getting at his girl. Hell his girl was trying to holler at me. I'm going to have to get me a gun for protection." Antwon expressed.

"Well a gun doesn't solve the problem. It only causes more caious. Besides people kill peole not guns. It's just metal without a human counterpart. Have you tried to talk to him. Tell him she's jocking you. She's the one he needs to check."

Poet remarked.

"No I haven't talked to him but until I do straighten this out, I don't want to run into him with nothing. He's stupid for this girl and not thinking rationally.

I'm not about to loose my life behind a silly girl." Antwon said.

"Someone has to be the bigger man about this situation. Before somebody is seriously hurt over bullshit. I just met you, I plan to spend a lot more time with you. I don't need you hurt. I need you healthy, pounding that meat to me."

Laughing out loud, Poet spoke.

"I'm not going to hide. This fool better get his girl straight and leave me out of it. Because if I wanted her I could of had her months ago. Besides I have a sexy mature Cougar I'm into." Antwon replied.

"You have to keep your head. You have a football career to think about.

College to finish and a lot more life to live; maybe he hasn't grown up yet. You have a lot to gain by not playing kid games. So you have to make the right choice for you. Don't let him guide your destiny." Poet said.

"I won't babe. I enjoy talking to you. You help keep me grounded. I had a mind to go to get him before he gets me. But I will do just as you said. It may not be as serious as all that. Thank you for the advice. I'll leave it alone unless it comes to me.

I will let you go for now. May I call you tomorrow." Antwon said.

"Yes." "You have a good night my sex chocolate toy. Until tomorrow." Poet said with a big smile.

"Goodnight Poet I hope you have heated dreams." Antwon said hanging up.

Poet could hardly sleep, She was worried about Antwon. Knowing he's a young man and they are hot headed. She tosed and turned till the wee hours of the morning.

Wanting to call or text she finally fell asleep. Afew days went by, poet worried Antwon was in trouble. She called, there was no answer. She texted him.

I pray you are OK, have a good day talk to you later. It read.

"Mom," Rena called out as she entered Poets house. "Have you heard from Antwon. I heard he got into a fight after the football game." Rena spoke with concern.

"No I haven't talked to him in a few days. He told me about this guy that has beef with him over a girl. I hope he is alright. I have been kinda worried about him." Poet remarked.

"He's alright. I saw him at the apartment a little while ago. He did not get hurt. He told me to tell you he'll call you later." Rena said.

The next day after work Poet went looking for Antwon. She still had not heard from him. Her worry was growing to panic. She needed to see Antwon. To no avail she didn't find him. So she returned home. She felt he would call when he was ready to talk.

A few nights later Poet was awakened by knocks. The knocks at the door grew louder and louder. Poet was startled and pissed. It's one A.M who the hell could this be.

"Who is it." She blurted as she neared the door.

"It's Antwon, Poet. I have something I need to tell you. I got into a little scuffle after the game." He pressed out.

Poet's demeanor changed, she had to see him. She let him in almost knocking him over with a huge hug. "Are you hurt. I heard about your incident.

I don't see any bruises or cuts." Poet said concerned as she probed his upper body.

"Babe I'm fine, he charged me up after the game. And I beat his ass down. I guess he thought I would be tired. But I was fired up. He swung, I swerved and planted a blow to the head. He fell and I never let him back on his feet. A few licks my whole team was pulling us apart. His girl was there, she told him she was hitting on me.

And I wasn't paying her any attention. So she couldn't help herself. She wanted me even more. He apologized to me and they left the field arguing.

He told me he wouldn't bother me again. Now that things were clearer and his head still ringing. It's over. I haven't called because I went out of town to get me a piece. My cousin James sold me one. Told me to watch that fool he maybe embarrassed even more now. So to be on the safe side I did what I had to."

"What are your coaches saying about the situation." She asked concerned.

"They had me checked out by the team doctor. They said I'm still eligible for first draft pick." He comforted her fears.

Poet grinned super big. "I'm so proud of you. Good Luck! I'm glad you are safe and in one piece. I've been worried. And you say I'm trouble. Damn young man, yo ass keeping me up at night." She told him seriously.

Chapter Four\Half

Prelude

Poetry And Dinner

Poet found herself wanting to protect, and keep Antwon safe. After all she had not gotten the goods yet. Damn is that all you can think about girl. The man going Through some things. Just be there for him. Give him words of wisdom, comfort him in his time of need. She told herself. At work Poet sat and wrote poems about Antwon.

The mini date they shared at the park came to mind. She giggled letting the words flow onto the paper:

Fresh and new, like a breath of air
The wind blew soft and slow

The sounds in the dark

A lighten bugs spark

The beating of two hearts

Sweet, soft, warm and alluring

The smell of every breath inviting

Will you consume me

Or I you

The spell is so inticing

A glow of the moon

Whispers in the ear

A breeze tells you fall is near

Smile once smile twice

A breath of fresh air is oh so nice

By: Poet Ellis

A few days went by. Poet invited Antwon to dinner. She planned a great meal. He told her he loved fried chicken wings, oven baked mac and cheese, and lemon cake with butter cream icing. She called him to confirm the date.

"Hello babe," Antwon spoke senually.

"Hello Antwon how did you know it was me? She asked

"I programmed your info into my phone, when your daughter gave it to me. I did not want to lose it. He replied.

"Well I got this idea that maybe we could have dinner together. I would like to prepare some of your favorite eats." She told him. "Is pussy on the menu!" He asked

"Well I Hadn't thought of that. Is that going to fill you up?" Poet asked shocked.

"It might." He said.

"Maybe it could be then." She responded grinning.

"No Poet seriously I would love to have dinner with you. I have not eaten a home cooked meal in a long time." Antwon told her.

"Good, Friday night around seven. She asked.

"Great, I'd be glad to join you. See you then. He replied happily. "O.K. see you then ." She remarked.

"The food was tasty Poet, it makes me think of home. Thank you." Antwon said wiping his mouth with a green silk cloth napkin. "You look ravishing in that dress."

"I hope you saved room for dessert." She replied while lifting the glass dome from the home made cake.

"Wow, that makes me feel special, you put a lot into this dinner. How can I make it up to you." He said.

"You enjoying it is good enough for me. It really wasn't much trouble at all.

Besides the way to a mans heart is through his stomach." Poet said with a smile.

Later that night Poet found herself writing about the event. She was so taken by it she wrote another poem This one about his eyes. It read:

Prelude

The Eyes

The eyes never lie, the windows to the soul

The eyes so beautiful as the sky

Their beauty to behold

I see your eyes, looking to fill the imagination

Fulfilling the mind, a hearts infactuation

The eyes never lie, for death there in nothing there

For life there is everything, to accomplish everywhere

So open or closed, random their colors

They all have tears to cry, the eyes never lie

By:Poet Ellis

Chapter Five

I May be Hooked

After a three month tease. Poet finally gave Mr. Sherman his chance. Poet never really took Antwon serious. Something was telling her that he was truly serious. Poet's mind told her one thing, but her body said fuck it. Her body tingled with thirst.

"Antwon I had a great time at dinner. I want to se you again. What are your plans for tomorrow." Poet spoke into the phone.

"I have practice from twelve to three. After that my day has just cleared up. Besides I dreamed about you last night. He said !

"Oh do tell." She said.

"I dreamed I was straddled your body, looking down into your dark brown eyes.

You were smiling while I sang to Jamie Fox song. SEX IS ON MY MIND. We were getting into a heated kiss when my alarm went off." Antwon cried. "I was really into it too. It seemed so real. Ms. Ellis you are taking over my sleep."

"I got an idea, I would love to hear you sing to me in person someday. Meet me at the Fairfield. I will text you the room number when I'm there." Poet told him.

"Will that be smoking or none smoking.

The lady behind the glass window asked. "Smoking please." Poet replied.

"Your room number is two-thirteen, upstairs, front side. Here is the key. Thank you." The lady said.

Poet clutched her goody bag while she took the flight of stairs to the room. She didn't want any of it's contents to be reveled till Antwon arrived. She entered the room, pressed a\c because it was hot in the room. She lit a cashmere wood glade scented candles to fragrance the stuffiness out. She went out to get ice for drinks.

Now she waited for Antwon.

She sent the text with a smiling face emoticon. He text back see you soon, Ms. Ellis.

Antwon blew warn breathes in between her blue jean inner thigh.

All over her covered pussy. Making Poet hot as a lava flow. Antwon had no idea what to expect. He wanted to taste Poets center spot. Lick the sweet nectar of honey, so sweet.

Poet was elated to be in the presence of this young man.

She let all of her inhabitations go. There was nothing standing in her way. They were behind closed doors. Alone. As Antwon massaged her body Poet flinched. It had been so long since she'd been touched in this manner.

Antwon,s large manly hands soft and caressing rubbed Poet's thighs and hips.

Shaking his head in disbelief of her thickness. His hands trembled with excitement.

He was actually touching her. Antwon didn't rush what he was doing which was getting his feel on.

Poet lay back upon the bed. Eyes half closed she whispered. "My other leg is getting jealous."

"Don't you worry I am getting to that side soon enough." Antwon whispered back. He asked Poet to turn around. She flipped until she was exactly the way he ordered her.

Poet smiled laying her head back. Antwon came up to kiss her lips. It was a long lingering kiss. He then kissed her breast, her waist then her knee. Before he began to massage her other leg. There was a college football game on the television.

He glanced at it trying to keep his head. That didn't work.

"May I taste you Poet. I just want to enjoy you, make you feel good. Every woman wants to feel good." Antwon said.

Poet raised her head and smiled. "You may." Was all she replied.

Antwon removed her black boots, placing them in the corner. He then loosed her belt with his teeth. Rubbing his hands up her outer thighs. He unbuttoned her jeans. Politely asked her to raise her hip so he could get them off. Poet grinned and obliged him. Antwon folded and placed each item in the chair next to the bed. While Poet lay there,

Antwon just looked for a moment. Taking in the scenery, he asked calmly, " May I?"

Poet nodded yes. Antwon removed her black and pink lace panties, while on his knees in front of her.

She watched as he folded them too. "Place them neatly over here, I know a lady likes to keep her stuff on point." Antwon remarked.

Antwon Sherman immediately went to Poet's sweetness. Slowly allowing his tongue to dance around. Poet squirmed without control. Antwon's tongue was hot between her legs.

"Shit!" Poet welted out, raising herself from the bed.

"Lay back babe, we're headed to another world." Antwon said smiling.

Antwon spread Poet legs and pressed his face closer to her. Kissing and licking her as if she was a tootsie roll candy piece.

He placed his fingers into her wetness. Poet was out of control now. His strong muscular arms grasped around her thighs. He locked on tight to keep her from running or squirming. He released one arm to shove her hand from his forehead.

Pulling his long braided hair was ok with him. But he didn't want Poet to push him away. Suddenly he stopped.

"Will you pull all of your clothes off. I want to enjoy everything."

Antwon replied.

Poet stood, did it sensually saying. "Now what?" Sitting back on the bed, Antwon peeled away his clothes throwing them anywhere.

She watched in amazement. This motherfucker is fine as all get out. She thought. There were muscles everywhere.

Her face lit up as Antwon walked to the bed. His penis hard, sticking out long and thick. His ass was like an apple, firm and smooth. It really stuck out.

Fine as frog hair. Poet thought. She stared. Antwon made sure she took in the full view. Magnum covering his big caramel stick he slowly pulled her to him.

Poet felt every pulsate as Antwon pushed for her depth. Oh God, she thought exhaling as he slowly entered her. Antwon inside got the feel.

He was getting comfortable with her. Things got heated. He kissed her passionately rubbing his hands through her hair.

"I love the hair." He whispered in her ear. Antwon began to long stroke her, his penis grew thicker, and longer.

Poet couldn't breathe. Damn it's good... She thought as she screwed him back. Antwon grabbed her huge breast in his hands, sucking her nipples like a hungry baby.

Poet moaned with delight. Antwon filled her every desire. She pushed and pulled him while she held on for dear life.

Poet felt Antwon moaning. He raised her from the bed never loosing track.

He bounced her on his piece like she was on a pogo stick.

Not knowing what to do, she knew she was on the clouds. Quivering as he came.

He still held her in the air. They both went falling upon the bed. "Oops! He laughed. While they both stared into each other eyes.

"Poet please don't let this age difference factor in on how you feel about me.

Can we do this again." He said.

"If it's no problem for you, its not a problem for me. We are indulging in each other's company for now." She replied.

Antwon scoot close behind her and squirmed. He wanted to taste her again. Yet she had a different idea. She softly grasped his penis. Stroking it made him groan.

This brought on an erection. Covering it again, Antwon lay back as Poet straddled him.

Poet contracted and released all the way down, then back up. He could feel all of it.

He bite his bottom lip, holding on to her thighs as she rode him with thrill.

A mechanical bull didn't have shit on her. Antwon was eating it up. "Push back!"

She whispered. He did just that.

"I had no idea the dream you told me about, would be me atop of you. Looking down into your eyes, talking about us actually doing what we're doing."

"It's like De Ja Vu, I am having a blast. I want you to let it go." He said.

Poet began to dismount him confused. He began to smile and told her not to stop. "I meant let that cum go. I want it all." He stated softly.

They continued to make love until he released yet again. Poet lay over blowing. Damn you got me shaking. You really are wild, I may be hooked!" Antwon remarked.

Chapter Six

Whipped

Poet met Antwon having no idea he would be an inspiring player in her life. She wrote poems about him from heated kisses and conversation. He tells her he's her sex toy. He also tells her he loves everything about her. Their conversations were very interesting.

She hadn't told anyone of their escapades. But she had wrote about them. That way she could get the excitement out. And know her secret was safe, here. Damn, he makes me murmur. Takes me to a fantasy place when he's between my legs face first.

"Come on, just like I told you. Sit on my face!" He says.

She of course did just that. It was great. Her sitting on his face. He says he can't believe it. Shit she couldn't either. This was their second rendezous and it still felt like a dream. When it was a dream she was hot and horney. Now that it's Reality, she's flabbergasted. Antwon really did her dirty both times. But she also did him in too.

Antwon shook, gasp, and bellowed out too. "Shit, damn and kept insisting how great she was. Girl you are damn good"

Poet decided to make him feel the same. She pushed all ladyness to the side, and freaky Poet came out. She kissed Antwon until she came upon his piece.

Blowing on him a warm breath. Rising to the occasion, Antwon up on his elbows watching. Poet looked into his eyes as she softly licked his job. Antwon eyes lit up like Christmas bulbs.

He could not have known Poet would go there. "If you are my sex toy I should play with you to the fullest." Poet said happily.

She then attacked Antwon as if he were her personal blow pop. Just as he began to breath heavy, Poet popped his piece out of her mouth with a plopping sound.

Climbing up on him she put him into her center. They both moaned with pleasure as she slide slowly down his huge shaft. Dropping his elbow position to holding Poets waist.

Antwon bite his bottom lip as his eyes rolled to the back of his head. "Shit girl you are good. Was all he could say. I had no idea how good this would be. And let me find out you freaky too!" He repeated.

"You just found out!" Poet smirked funly.

They both grinned having fun, breathing hard and uttering sexual inundos at each other.

Abruptly Antwon stops and say's he needs a square because he is in shock and awe.

Trying to lit it up, he has a difficult time getting the lighter to work. He's shaking .

I actually have him shaking. Damn I'm good! Poet thought to herself. A few quick puffs he quickly put it out. "Can you stand up and bend over."

Poet stood but she didn't bend. She didn't play that butt thang. Not knowing what he wanted to do she just glanced back at him. He was staring. "You have more ass than Janet Jackson." He remarked

Poet smiled saying "AS if you've seen Janet Jackson ass in person."

Antwon still staring began to stroke himself. " I'm embeddind this picture into my memory bank. Poet began to think doggie style. When she felt Antwons tongue, it was hot and fierce. Lick, Lick, Lick he indulged her from behind. Poet was floored. As she leaned into the wall with her head back mouth wide the fuck open.

Antwon was enjoying everything. Placing kisses upon her cheeks Antwon rose to his feet. Inviting himself to the party. Thrusting as if he was pulling roots.

Antwon threw his head back shaking it back and forth. She could hear the beads on his long braided hair clacking together. Changing positions he placed her on the bed edge and held her up.

Climbing on top as if he were building a wooden box. Antwon downed Poet until they both saw stars.

"Shit that was hot!" He replied. "I have never been done like that. What have you done to me? I'm whipped, And shaking. May I have another smoke. You got me smoking and I don't even smoke."

Crashing to the floor Antwon's legs had given out. They both laughed out loud. They lay talking He on the floor and she on the bed.

Poet looking down at his body. Damn he's a fine young tender that was stuck on her. She was stuck on him too. Apple shaped ass, muscles everywhere, even his muscles had muscles.

It's a myth, working out does not make the meat shrink At least not in his case.

Poet thought.

Another hour passed they both knew they needed to go home. But it was almost as if they didn't want to go.

"Your going to depart without giving me a kiss." Antwon Sherman remarked as Poet began to exit the room. She closed the door back, they began to kiss passionately embracing one another.

Pulling apart she whispered, " I know we have to go. But keep this up and we will be back right back in that bed."

"I do know it!" Antwon remarked excitedly. "You have a good night Poet." "You do the same." Poet replied closing the door ending their night.

Poet grinned all the way home, two a.m. in the morning. Wishing she would have stayed, could have stayed, wanted to stay. She would never over do him. Let what happened soak into the both of their brains. Somebody pinch me Please. She thought.

Chapter Seven

Away Too Long

Poet slowly came down from hae adreneline rush. Antwon Sherman had a hold on her. She could barely work. Antwon was taking over her thoughts. She stumbled over things. She even bumped her head a couple of times. This has to stop…..Poet thought. The next few days Poet found herself struggling with her phone. She was checking it every few minutes, to see if a new text was waiting. None, Nota, Nothing.

Now her mind was telling her call him, text him. But she refused, thinking let him make the first move. After all she didn't want to look desperate. The heat between her legs made her call. No answer. Antwon was at school, she had forgotten he was a college student.

Later that night Poet's phone beeped. It was Antwon sending a text.

Hello, Poet I have been thinking of you like crazy. I didn't want to let you go the other night.. I'm your sex toy use me up. A. Sherman.

Poet laughed out loud. She sent one back. Hey you, LOL, I 've been waiting on your call. Been thinking bout you too…Smiles Poet.

They sent messages back and forth for awhile. Hot racey messages.

After twelves days she was overdue. She needed a sexual fix bad. Antwon had her ditzy. He was all she could think about. The way his lips felt between her thighs. How his muscular body was so firm and smooth. She thought about the next time she would see him. Wanting to hug him, feel his body in her arms. Antwon Sherman had been away too long.

Wednesday afternoon He called.

"Hello babe, I would love to see you. Are you busy. Antwon spoke into the phone.

Poet grinned answering, "Hey Mr. Sherman, you sound so good, what did you have in mind."

I'm at home, I want you to see my new place. We can catch a movie." He said.

"O.K., give me the directions. I will be there shortly." Poet replied. She scrambled to fix herself up. She was a nervous wreck. She was good with directions, but in her haste she got lost. She drove around killen for fifteen minutes. She didn't want Antwon to think she was not capable of finding him. After passing the same store four times she decided to stop and ask someone. The first guy Hispanic, didn't speak English.

She drove quickly through a trailer perk. Going over high speed bumps, she was forced to slow down. There was another man walking. Poet pulled over and asked him. He told her she was across the street from her destination. She just shook her head in disbelief. "Thank you." Poet remarked. As she turned into the town homes Antwon was waving so she could find the right place.

"Please come in. This is my bachelor pad. How are you, thanks for coming." He said.

"Hi you I'm great. I got lost but I'm here now that's all that counts. You have a lovely place. The things we do to see someone." Poet replied.

They sat talking and begin to enjoy a movie. Only a movie was far from either of their minds.

Chapter Eight

Third Times A Charm

His Place

Poet And Antwon were getting very close. He told her he was great at cooking, loved kids, and eating pussy, especially hers.

Poet listened smiling, letting him do the most talking. This was the gateway to learning all about him. He was fasinating. It made her feel like she was on clouds as he talked about her.

"Can I offer you something to drink. I have Pierre, Fiji, and A@w rootbeer soda.

I don't have anything strong, it's almost training season." He told her.

"Yes some Fuji will be fine. Sitting in close proximatey has me heated inside." Poet spoke. "You excite me and I can not help myself.

Antwon gently grabbed her hand, leading her to his bedroom. "This is my quiet sanctuary, thinking spot. Pleae have a seat." He spoke turning the I-pod home on. "You like jazz and R&B. Let me make you comfortable." He knelt to remove her thong sandals.

"Thank you." Poet replied.

Antwon disappeared down a long low lit hall. Poet heard him singing. She grinned looking around. Black comforter trimmed in silver draped the queen size bed. Huge pillows line the head of it. No pictures adorn the walls. There were box upon box stacked with Nike shoes in the corner. Things neatly placed. Poet sat still until he reappeared.

Clap, Clap! Antwon gestered as he spoke bluntly. "You know how I like it, Pull those jeans off."

Poet didn't waste time as she removed her jeans. Antwon just stared. "You are wearing my new favorite color. Those red and gold thongs are banging." He said dropping to his knees kissing her covered spot. "You smell so damn sweet babe. That's why I can't get enough of it. It calls me all the time."

Poet said nothing, hypnotized and speechless once again.

Antwon removed Poet's panties. "I'm giong to keep these!" He snickered as he latched on to her hot spot. Poet decended to the bed. Straightened her arms out,

as if she were about to run. He locked his arms around her thighs, and went to work.

Poet could hear him breathing heavy. "You should come up for air." She told him.

Trying to break the suction. "That's no fair, holding me down. I can't take it." Poet squirmed and scooted going absolutely nowhere.

Antwon held a firm grip. She thought his face was stuck in her sugar jar. He finally rose, chin hairs milky wet. "You let go babe, shit that's what I'm talking bout. The nectar is hella sweet!" He said licking his lips with a devilish smile.

She didn't waste any time. She put her left hand in his chest. Pushed him against the wall. She dropped to a squat while placing her right hand on Antwon's stick.

Poet flicked his penis with her tongue. He moaned in delight. She was on fire and planned to take it out on him. Poet placed Antwon into her mouth. She slowly worked it.

His breathing became loud. She wanted him to enjoy this meeting too. She looked into his face, he had the sexiest sex face. He was looking down at her dreamy eyes while biting on his bottom lip.

"Shit babe it's so damn good." He finally uttered out, As his legs began to quiver.

Poet stopped just close to making Antwon burst off. Antwon gasped a few times as Poet released him. He quickly spent her around. "Babe I want to do you doggie style."

He told her. Antwon dipped into her passion spot. He pounded with fierce force. "I'm going to explode! He yelled, and did just that.

Chapter Nine

Let The Fun Begin

Mid-October the weather getting cooler forced Poet to work longer days. She missed spending time with a Antwon. She lay across her California king with her eyes closed.

Trying not to call him. He being young she knew his life was fast paced. She worked hard coming home to nothing. She thought what it would be like if she and Antwon could be together more. She daydreamed about them enjoying some life together. She also had the thought of their ages. She knew there was no way they would be anything more than sexual friends. Poet thought to much. She was trying to talk herself out of anything further. She didn't want her heart broken. She felt him being younger he had plenty of life to live. He wasn't trying to be tied down. No matter how great of a time they had. Poet decided to let the chips fall where they may. She was feeling Antwon Sherman. Giving him up was not an option right now. They began to open up about their past. They were getting to know each other very well. Going to lunch, dinner, and a couple of times she cooked. It made her feel good to know Antwon cared about her.

He made her feel like a women who was new to anything. She found herself smiling all day, because she thought of Antwon. He was giving her what she needed. And she was getting what she wanted. So let the fun begin! She thought, preparing for bed.

Chapter Ten

Daydream

As Poet backed out of her driveway, she noticed her car wasn't going backwards fast enough. She placed the KIA in park and got out. "Damn a flat." She spoke out loud.

As she fixed her flat poet thought that's another reason she needed a man around. She began to daydream Antwon was changing her tire. The sun beamed across his topless shoulders. Sweat rolled down the center of his back. His khaki cargo shorts lay just above his peeping crack. Poet stood watching with sexual fantazies dancing in her head.

Come back Poet You need to get to work....She thought. She grinned as she tightened the bolts on the dummy tire. She threw the flat in the trunk to get fixed later. Cleaned her hands with GoJo. Rinsed with the outside water hose and she went on about her day. Antwon,

Antwon, Antwon, She wrote all over her napkins at lunch. He was on the brain. That was for sure. The Thanksgiving holiday was coming. Poet began to make preparations for the day. She loved to cook on the holidays. Even more she enjoyed family and togetherness. This was another reason to have her house full. Maybe Mr. Sherman will visit. She thought with a smile.

Chapter Eleven

Revealed Feelings

Poet home was huge She was having a great time. There were at least fifty people wondering through her place. A knock arose at the door. "Come In." Everyone watching the game yelled. It 's Antwon. Poet wanted to melt. She smiled big. Antwon hugged her tightly. The Kenneth Cole "Black" She got him was captivating. He wore dark black jeans, a sky blue sweater vest trimmed in black, with black Sperry Ellis shoes. He was swagged out. He wasn't dressed like a typical twenty-one year old man. But he was popping eyes all through the house.

Poet took notice that everything she touched she dropped, knocked over, or spilled.

Antwon made her silly nervous. She couldn't think straight when he was around. "Poet how is your day going?" Antwon asked.

"Even better now that your here." She spoke sheepishly. " You look great."

"You got my meat hard. You know you didn't have to wear those black leather pants. I love the whole essemble. Your shirt is leaving silver glitter specks everywhere. Will I have some on me." Antwon said with a smile.

"Keep that up you are going to get some all over you right now." Poet remarked as she laughed aloud.

Poet began to mingle through the crowded house. She didn't want to over indulge Antwon. Let him breath some. Even though she wanted to jump his bones. Kick everybody out. Fuck it. She didn't though. Antwon stayed until everyone was gone. He wanted to talk. Sitting across the room from each other. Antwon began to spill out.

"Poet I am not sure I should be saying any of this. But I must, It's weighing heavy on me. I'm infatuated with you. Your a wonderful woman I'm glad I met you. Even more grateful we have gotten to know each other. I'm getting feelings for you. I never thought I would fall so fast. Your good to me and good for me. I must confess some things to you. Before the family reunion I felt as though I already knew you.

Well knew of you anyway. Roger was telling me about you. About how sexy your eyes were. How good you looked. He even told me you were toteing a huge ass on your back. I was already aware of your age. Everything you could imagine I knew. He told me you were single and lived alone. Every time he visited Rena, he came back and filled me in. I was so intrigued I had to see for myself. I had no intentions of anything, except that, when I laid eyes on you. Honestly I was glad he invited me to come with him to meet the family. He didn't want to come alone." Antwon explained.

"O.K. But there were plenty of young women there. Why me? I was under the impression that you were an item with Nasha, Rena's friend .

It looked as though she was eyeing you like a bodyguard. That's why I did not take you seriously. I don't have time to be at odds with anyone over someone who isn't interested in me." She replied.

"Poet I'm sure I could have persued any one of the young women there, that was throwing themselves at me. But you were the challenge. You weren't paying me any attention. At least not the kind I wanted anyway. I love a challenge. I can get ass on any corner. Yet a women who preserves herself, now that's a rare find.

When we left, It was my idea to come back for the food. I wanted then to say something so badly. I had to build up my nerves. I also wanted to see if you would inquire about me." He told her looking deep into her eyes.

"I heard you were asking about me. I didn't want to be made a fool of, so I waited. Curious and slow to jump into anything. Besides I rarely make the first move. I wanted you to be sure of your pursuit." Poet explained. "And look at us now, I'm happy things happened the way they did."

"So am I babe. So am I." He said. They talked into the early morning. "Oh Poet I'm sorry, it's very late and you got work. I had better excuse myself. May I visit you later. Antwon said.

"Sure I've enjoyed your company, your always welcome to stop by. You drive safely."

She told Antwon as she closed the door. Knock, knock, Poet opened the door.

Antwon leaned in and kissed her on the lips. "I forgot to give you that, good night babe."

"Awe baby that was sweet of you." She replied closing the door again. She stood there for a moment basking in the glory.

65

Chapter Twelve

Excitement And Sadness

Good afternoon class I'm your substitute teacher Mrs. Helman. "Antwon Sherman," she called out. While taking the roll. There was chatter over the intercom. Antwon was struggling with the fact of telling Poet he was leaving soon.. He wasn't focused. "Antwon Sherman," she repeated. The coach has called you to the football field immediately. Confused Antwon excused himself from class.

"Coach you wanted to see me." Antwon asked.

"Yes I do son. Step over here with me for a minute." The coach said. As they walked to the side line the coach placed his arm across Antwon's shoulders. "Son I'm going to miss the hell out of you. I have been informed the Colts want you."

He then yelp loudly. "I knew you were destin for greatness the first time I laid eyes on you. Congratulations!"

Antwon was estatic. "Your kidding me coach." Antwon shouted excited. "I have dreamed of this moment all of my life."

Antwon pushed out alligator tears falling from his eyes. He was so elated he jumped on his coach and hugged him tight. "Thank you.!"

"There will be a press conference on Tuesday of next week.

That will give your family time to get here. You finally have arrived kid. Go get em!" The coach said.

Antwon thought he was going to boot camp. But he was about to be drafted, to the Indianapolis Colts. His favorite team. He could hardly believe it himself.

"Practice is over here, no boot camp, you are headed for the big league. Once again, I'm so happy for you Antwon." The coach said.

Headed back to pack his locker he thought… I thought it was going to be hard to tell Poet I'm going to boot camp in a month. But now I'm telling her I will be leaving for the NFL in less than thirty days. Happiness and sorrow go hand and hand. Now he was really thinking.

Just tell her maybe she'll understand. I hope she will. This is a very important time in my life. Antwon needed to think. He was so excited he wanted to tell her right away. But he was feeling sad because he and her were getting to the really falling for each other stage.

Chapter Thirteen

Presedence

Football takes over Sherman's life. Poet begans to withdraw. She had not seen Antwon in weeks. She felt as if something was missing. And it was. Antwon. "Hello, Poet. I have missed you so. I've been subject to nothing but stale manly smells." Football camp has been rough but it's over." "I need you." Antwon spoke softly from the other end of the phone line.

Poet agreed. She missed him too. All she thought about was him. Looking into his steamy gray eyes. Kissing his soft lips. "Your welcome to come by." Poet remarked.

As they embraced each other. They held on as if someone were trying to pull them apart.

"Poet we need to talk. Please lets sit. I have news you aren't going to like." Antwon said. Poet sat looking with a confused look upon her face.

"Poet I have grown to care about you. I never thought I would have met a woman like you. I have enjoyed spending time with you. My heart has also gotten heavy with fondness for you. Antwon expressed as he placed his hand upon his cheeks. I have been drafted to play for the Indianapolis colts. I leave in three weeks. Im sorry. Football is my dream. It takes precedence over all.

I hope we can keep in touch. I have no idea how long training camp will take. Once it's over we could at least text and call each other." He explained.

Poet was floored, as the hurt began to set in. She took a deep breathe then spoke.

"Antwon you are a great guy. I too have developed feelings. I don't want to lose what we have. I will not stand in the way of your dream." Poet spoke as a tear drop fell down her face. She felt her heart hecome heavy. I also knew this day would come. I am so happy for you." She replied sulling.

Kissing the tear drop as it slide down her cheek, Antwon just looked deeply into her glossy eyes. "I will come back for you Poet. I won't forget you. I promise. Antwon remarked with tears swelling in his eyes as well.

"You get to Indianapolis and it's audious Poet. There are beautiful women all over.

You won't have time to think about me. I will miss you terribly. I do understand.

I'm grateful to have met you. It won't be easy, But I will be ok. Maybe keeping in touch wouldn't be such a good idea. I won't ruin your life. You have plenty of of life left. Go kick some ass. Be all you can babe.!" Poet replied, as more tears fell..

Antwon wrapped his strong arms around her. He felt sorrow too. Over whelmed with joy about his career. Yet sad he would have to leave Poet. They sat quietly holding one another till dawn. Trying to be strong about the situation, Poet cooked Antwon breakfast.

Eating in silence they both knew three weeks would pass fast.

"Let's enjoy this time together babe. This doesn't have to be a sad good-bye.

All good-byes aren't gone good-byes. Antwon spoke.

"I would so enjoy that. I really don't have a choice Love it' set it free. Like it' let it be. I can deal." Poet spoke as her lips quivered.

Antwon grabbed her hand, spun her into his massive chest. Placing a gentle kiss on her forehead. "This is hard enough already Poet." "I love you!" Antwon blurted out.

Poet's mouth fell open. With bucked eyes she asked, "What did you say?" "You heard me Poet, I said it." "I LOVE YOU!!" I had to tell you before I leave. "How i'm feeling deep within." Antwon expressed.

No Smiling, Poet cries out "I Love You!! Too babe. Both smiling having gotten that off their chest. They hugged and Antwon had to go. "Good-Bye Poet." Antwon Pushed out.

"Good-Bye Mr. Sherman." Poet also pushed out.

Chapter Fourteen

Always Remember

Poet sulled for weeks. Antwon was on the brain. Work began to get better. She filled her days with long hours. She passed on hanging out with friends. She wanted Antwon Sherman. They had not talked in months. I have got to pull myself together. Poet thought.

Post season football began Monday night, Dallas Grandstanders vs. Indianapolis Colts. Are Ya ready for some Football. Came blarring out of the tv.

Poet's facial expression changed from sour grapes, to sweet watermelon. She knew she was going to see Antwon.

She started walking around singing. Antwon is giong to be on tv. Antwon is going to be on tv. Poet knew as long as Antwon played professional ball, she would Always remember him. As well as be able to see her Everything pleaser.

She called her daughter Rene.

"Hey come watch the game with me. My special guy is playing tonight. "Mom I would love to, but I got work. Maybe next time.

Besides I don't want to see you melting away watching tv."Rene replied laughing. "Ha! Ha!, Rene very funny. You know I miss Antwon terribly. I let him go. I at least want to see him if nothing else. This way I will always remember the great times we shared together." Poet said with a huge smile.

"Mom cook your wings and enjoy the game. Are shall I say, Gauck at the screen. We will talk later. Love you! Good-Bye." Rene burst out as she hung up the phone.

It wasn't five minutes into the game. There he is. Running onto the field, His name being called by Tony Dorsett. "Antwon Sherman # 5, wide reciever for the Indianapolis Colts. #1 draft pick from Killen, Texas. Won the Heiser trophy last year. He is the favorite to keep your eyes on."

Poet sat watching the screen with her mouth wide open. Glad she decided to watch. Antwon looked damn sexy in his shiny purple football pants. His hair draped over his shoulder pads. Only Poet could make football be sexy. She sat glued till the game was over. Beside the cold shower did not help. The sight of him had her brewing.

Poet's phone rang, waking her from a deep sleep. She glanced at the clock. It was three thirty am.

"Hello Poet, It's Antwon." "How are you." His voice came slowly through the reciever.

"Hello Antwon, Im a hell of a lot better now that I hear your voice!" "I catch every game, that way I can see you. Keep up with your well being. You look so damn scrumptious out there on the field." She remarked.

"Poet I'm having a great time here. It's everything I dreamed of and so much more. I hoped to live this dream for a long time!" Antwon replied.

Poet got quiet. "Antwon I miss you, Squeezing those apple ass cheeks. The way your jaws light up when you smile." "With your sexyness." "How are they treating you."

"Great I hope." "Tell them don't make me come out there and kick some asses." She said playfully.

"I'll make a note of that. They are treating me very well. I sent you a package in the mail. It should be there in a day. I hope you enjoy it. Well I have to go now Love. Hope to talk to you soon. Sleep tight." Antwon said as he hung up the phone.

"Goodnight Antwon." Poet replied as she spoke into the beeping line. Poet couldn't sleep thinking about what it could be he was sending in the mail. When she got to work she was bomb rushed by a few co-workers. They were all beaming with curiosity. Chanting who is he, who is he. Not fully aware of what they meant, she opened her office door.

There were dozens upon dozens of red and white roses.

There must of been twenty dozen. One adorn a giant card. Poets mouth dropped. "Who is he, who is he, her co-workers were still chanting as she closed the door. She wanted to read the card privately. She knew they were from Antwon. And began to smile. Her heart thumped almost out of her chest. Poet opened the card. It read: I told you I would never forget you. Your Sex Toy!! There was number three circled in the corner. What does that mean Poet thought. What a very thoughtful surprise.

Lunch came quickly. Poet went home elated about her suprising morning.

Checking her mail as she did everyday at lunch time. There was another letter. It read: Poet here is something for you to enjoy. Please wear it when you sleep. Think of me. There was a smaller envelope inside that instructed her to go to her daughters and pick up the package that arrived special delivery.

Poet didn't go inside for lunch. She headed straight to her daughters. Rena wasn't there but she left a note on her door. Mom key under mat, gift on table. See you tonight when you get off! Rena. Poet didn't think anything of it. But her excitement level began to rise. She rushed inside to get her box.

The box was neatly wrapped in silver glossy foil of wrapping paper. A huge multi colored bow on top neatly tied. She quickly ripped at the paper. Inside was a jersey with the number five on it, with his signature:Antwon Sherman. There was another envelope.

It read: My blood sweat, and tears on it. I send this to you because I want you to be close to me always. I LOVE YOU!!! C U SOONER? With the number two circled.

Poet sniffed the collar of the garment. She could smell Kenneth Cole's Black as well as Antwon as if he were right there in the room with her. She boxed her goodies, placed them in the front seat and returned to work. She called Rena to tell her she got the gift and where to retrieve her key. There was no answer.

Voicemail. So she sent a quick text. With all the beautiful flowers in her office her day seemed to go by fast.

Four thirty p.m. Rena called her.

"Hello mom, How has your day been today." She asked happily.

"It's been very interesting, first I get an office fulll of roses. At lunch I get a shinny wrapped gift. I have been in the clouds all day." Poet said out ou joy. "I have been instructed to tell you to give all the flowers to your co-workers except a dozen red and a dozen white. Bless someone else with a little joy as well." Rena said.

"Ok Rena what is this all about. You are talking crazy." She replied.

"No, mom that's what I was told to tell you to do. Now I will see you a little later.

Love you mom got to go! Click.

Poets coworkers were glad to get the flowers. A couple of the guys said "Im taking my wife out to dinner tonight and going to give these to her." "Maybe I can get Lucky."

Them not knowing they were really from a famous football player. Poet smiled and waved as she left for the day.

Chapter Fifteen

All On The Table

Poet entered her home removing her seven inch heels, headed up stairs to get her house shoes. There was a note taped to the wall. Beyond these stairs your final gift awaits. Poet ran up the steps At the top was another note you are close to your hearts desire this note read. She opened her bedroom door rose petals were all over the floor. Candles burned with an inviting aroma. Another envelope sat propped up on her pillow. She grabbed it and opened it. Its said for you I will. Look behind you!!! It had the number one on it.

Poet turned around to see another standby in the doorway. She ran to him and stretched wide with tears in her eyes.

Antwon it's you. How did you do this. Poet cried as she held him tightly Antwon said nothing, he just held her tightly too. He just wanted to feel her breathe upon his neck. Feel her heart beating against his chest.

"Poet I have missed you so much I wanted to surprise you. Rena helped me.

She ordered the flowers, wrapped the gift, and sneaked here and fixed all this up for you/us. I wrote the letters and placed them myself." "Hello Baby"! He remarked excitedly "Come lets go down stairs, dinner is waiting for you!!"

Poet was speechless. She just held Antwon's hand and let him lead her. The kitchen had candles lite as a center piece. A bottle of Don on ice. Two silver dome covers, placed closed together. The chairs were also close.

"I don't want to sit far away. I want to be as close as possible." "You don't mind do you." Antwon asked.

"No."Poet replied as she sat in the chair he pulled out for her. The food was gourmet prepared.

Poet was taken away. Trying to wrap her head around all the events of the day. Now to be sitting eating dinner with Antwon. What a day. I will never forget this. She thought smiling.

"Baby I plan to pamper you." "Enjoy you to the fullest." "Make this a night to remember for the both of us." "So relax and come alone to some contemporary Blues.

They both had a Blues fetish. It was breed in their souls. Sitting so close Poets temperate began to rise. She wanted to put her body on the table.

"I have a surprise for you upstairs." "Lets get a couple of glasses and meet at the bathroom door." Antwon spoke softly.

"You've been a busy little beaver. Thank you, I am enjoying this/ you to the fullest." Poet replied grinning big. Standing at the door Poet let him open it.

The lighting was low. Bubble creeping off the sides of the tub. The scent of sandlewood and ocean breeze captivated her nose. There were Roses and lilies this time. The 2 dozen she brought were now placed in a walking path petal style, with the lilies on the outside. He also place one across the middle. Seven spaced out to look like square flower boxes. He put the glasses at the edge of the tub, sat the ice chilled wine and bucket beside them.

Antwon turned to Poet. He began to undress her. Slowly removing her blouse. He kissed each of her breast. He then unbuttoned her pants kneeling down to kiss her navel. Pulling her pants completely to the floor. Poet stepped out of them as Antwon released her of them. Then he held her hips where her bikini line stopped. He just stared at her chocolate toned under ware. Poet stood looking down at him and said nothing. She was soaking it up."I'm just taking a mental photo baby." "I want you." Antwon replied before he placed a kiss on her covered pussy. He then stood up removing her panties while easing down her body until he was face to face with what he ached for. On his way back up he lifted her off her feet. Snuggly in his arms he lowered her body into the water.

He then left her to freshen up. Telling her, "I'll meet you in the bedroom. "A silk robe is hanging there for you."

Poet didn't know what to say. She was still wrapping her mind around it.

All of this for me. How caring and thoughtful. She pondered.

Chapter Sixteen

The Things They Did to One Another

Poet emerged from the bath. She didn't dry off she put on a short burgundy robe. Slipped on her house shoes and meet Antwon in the bedroom. Antwon sat at the foot of the massive bed. "Damn you smell good baby, he said. He stood and picked Poet up again. He eased into the bed placing Poet in the center of it. Removing her robe. "Can I look at you baby." "I want to feel you all over." "This baby oil should do the trick. Antwon squirted the baby oil into the palm of his hand. Rubbing them together. Drops of baby oil fell upon Poets skin. Making her jump.

He placed his warm hands on her moist body. His hands found her breast then her neck and arms. Antwon massaged every inch of her.

He parted her legs and felt Poet quivers. He rubbed close to her spot. It tickled her fantasy. Poet lay almost lifeless.

His strong muscular hands explored with tight grips then soft ones. Everywhere.

He began to kiss her body, every other kiss his tongue touched her skin.

Poets body jumped, shivered, and tightened up. Antwon was emotionally pleasing her.

Poet couldn't hardly take it any more. She attempted to make moves of her own. "No, Baby." "I want to do you," Antwon said. "You Got That Kind Of Love" by Levert, came blaring from the CD that was playing.

"Damn that's my song." "I hear it and it make me think of you." he replied he song softly with the music.

Antwon began to gaze into Poets eyes. He firmly gripped his dick, shaking it back and forth. Letting the head peep in and out of his closed palm. While he aroused him self, he moved his fingers in Poets hot, moist, pussy.

She moaned in pleasure. Her eyes watched every move he was making. Her body was waited and on fire. Her moistness began to flow.

Antwon knew it to. He placed his juicy lips on her pussy. Kissing it as if saying, Hello I missed you too. Poet's mouth opened in amazement. Antwon had her floating. It felt as if her body came off the bed. Antwon's mouth and fingers attacked Poets heated spot. She couldn't be still.

Antwon knew he had her right where he wanted her. Hot as fire. He mounted here, going deep. He hadn't felt Poet in a long time. He was thinking of all the things they did to one another. It was a driving force. He began to long stroke her. Moaning himself. Spewing words randomly. "Damn you feel good! This pussy is hotter than lava." "I can feel you cumming all on this dick."

"Oh yes! Baby I feel you on that. I love it when you speak soft, and dirty to me. You have out done yourself over and over again today." Poet remarked. "I am loving it."

Antwon groans began to get louder. He pressed against her body thrusting deep. His penis stiffened tightly as he blew his stack. Bellowing "I'm cumming!! Damn im cumming Poet! All he could do was lay upon her cottony warm body. Trying to come down off the roller coaster ride. They could feel each others heart throbbing as he lay his head upon her shoulder. After a few moments he rolled over, resting beside her. They body's synchronized in slowing breathes till they fell asleep. They were both drained.

Chapter Seventeen

Not Another Goodbye

Poet mumbled as she slapped the alarm clock. She began to focus on her room, it was still decorated out. She lay smiling when she realized Antwon was not there. "Antwon." She called out, "Are you still here. Last night was incredible!" There was a quiet silence. Poet knew he was gone. She smiled as she replayed the last twenty four hours.

Time for work Poet, she told herself out loud. She crept to the bathroom because her body was aching. She needed a hot bubble bath to revive. She dressed and made her way down stairs. Her legs were still heavy. So it was challenging to get them working with the stairs. As she closed the fridge door, there was a note. That fell from out of nowhere.

It read:

Dear Poet

I had the best time of my life last night. I have your scent all over me. I didn't want to wake you this morning.

You looked as though you needed some serious rest ☺ I have to be back in Indianapolis tonight.☹, practice tomorrow. I'm sorry I couldn't explain. But I don't know when I will see you again. I just couldn't bring myself to see you with tears in your eyes. Its hard to pull away from you.

I wanted to enjoy you with no conviction. I Love You Poet. I miss you already.

Love Antwon (Your Sex Toy)

P.S. Until that day, Poet! XOXO

Poet held the letter close to her heart. Not another goodbye she thought. She dragged to work. She sobbed because she knew she would never see him again. She smiled to herself thinking, at least he out did himself. She even grimaced because her legs and body were whipped. Poet thought about Antwon for months. She yearned to just hear his voice. She took extra work so she wouldn't be able to see the games. She loved Antwon, and knew she had to love him from afar. She even expected she wouldn't see him again. Ever. Poet began to not hurt so bad about Antwon. She was happy for him. Besides she knew this day was coming. She just didn't know when.

Antwon had left Poet with good memories. Great ones to be exact. Poet eventually began to get back on the right track. She decided she would take a friends advice.

"It's been two years Poet, You have got what it takes to get a good man."

Her coworker told her. Poet took her time opening up to someone else. She didn't want a repeat, She had experienced love and lost. She just wanted to love and be loved again. She went on a few blind dates, Her friends fixed up for her.

The first man seemed obsessive. She never called him again. The second man was an athlete. She just couldn't bring herself to date him for fear he would leave too. And the last one was an older man. He peaked her interest. They talked all night long. There were a lot of common denominators they shared. She didn't ever want to forget Antwon Sherman. But she needed a life. One she could share love, her life, her forever with. She choose door number three. She could move on now. They began to date heavily. Time didn't stand still. She and her new guy Had gotten close. Wedding bells were being spoken up. Poet thought about Antwon from time to time. She would write letters and never send them. She wanted to let him live and enjoy life.

"Poet's getting married!" Her co worker cried with excitement.

"It's been a long road. I'm glad to see your happy again. Congrats!"

Poet was beaming, and excited to tell of her great fortune. She was finally on her way to marriage. She decided to throw herself a party, so she could tell her friends, and show off the new beau. As well as meet his family and friends. Everyone got along great. Rena was ecstatic about it. And that made Poet secure.

"Mom I'm happy for you! I knew there was someone out there for you. Yeah! My moms getting married. Rena yelped, as she spoke privately to her mother. "Yes, I need this! I need him! I Love Him!."

I still have dreams and thoughts of Antwon. But I know Royre Johnson is the right one for me." Poet expressed to Rena. "I'm so excited!!

They hugged with a joyful embrace. "Let's get back to the party. We are having a celebration aren't we?" Rena said.

"We sure are!" Poet said smiling.

Chapter Seventeen and a Half

Crystal Blue Waters

With the wedding fast approaching. Poet had a gang of things to get done. The florist designed water crest lilies, pink dyed roses, and perennials in beautiful arrangements. Her bouquet also had the same design.

Rosie Joplin Hall was decorated in black, white and gold. The streamer that hung from the ceiling ascended down over each table. There was a scented candle placed in the center of each table. There was a large candle placed in the center of each as well.

The tables were covered in round black silk cloths. A smaller white square silk cloth on top of that. Which made each table look like a tuxedo. There were also dark chocolate chip drops with the bottom dipped in gold lined to resemble buttons.

Each chair was draped in the same design only they were fancy tied in the back. White china lined with gold also adorn a smaller solid black plate atop. Abbot silver ware perfectly placed. With a personal card named for correct seating..

Each napkin had Poet and Royre embroidery deep into their thickness: They were tri folded. Pink and white rose petals were sprinkled all over the floor.

The aisle in the center had creamy white carpet. At the ends two huge African Vases were standing, with giant African Violets running over their tops.

In the front of the hall where the happy couple were to sit . There was a ten by twelve photo of them. They were on the island of Maui. There was a light beige sandy backdrop, the crystal blue water cascaded onto it.

Chapter Eighteen

A Phone Call

Poet you have a phone call on line one. You can take it in the brides dressing room. A church member informed her. Poet knew everyone she knew was sitting in the pews of the wedding chapel.

Who could this be she thought, As she answered the call. "Hello this is Poet, who ever this is you are late. The wedding will start in twenty minutes." She joyfully spoke into the receiver.

"Hello Poet!" The masculine voice replied back. I wanted to wish you the best. I'm so happy for you! Congratulations baby. Tell him he had better be better than good to you. He doesn't want me to have to come there. Antwon said with a sad slow demeanor. He then laughed softly saying. "No seriously, babe I ain't mad at you live your life. I'll always be in the background. Forever. I Love You Poet!

The line suddenly went dead. Poet stood without expression after all it had been four years since she last saw or heard from Antwon Sherman Her "COLLEGE MAN". Her sex toy. She smiled with a tear drop falling from her eye. She felt Antwon would always be a part of her life, her past.

She finished getting ready. Walking down the aisle she was so beautiful.

The groom was handsome and willing to have her as his own. And Poet Ellis was happy with that.

She wouldn't look back. But the call made her reflect. HMMM!